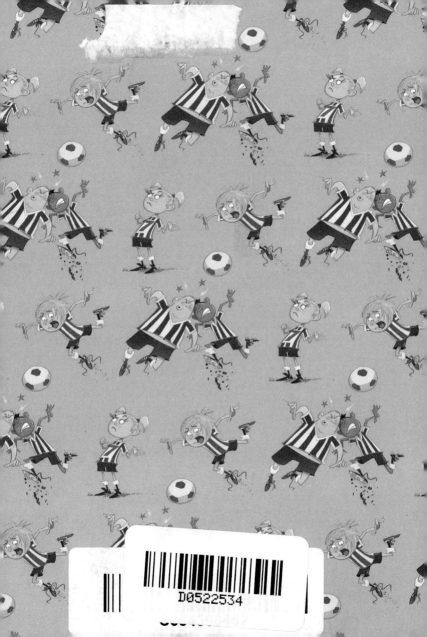

For my son, *Stan of the Saints*.

Proud of you pal ...

THE UNLUCKY ELEVEN

PHIL EARLE

With illustrations by Steve May

Barrington Stoke

First published in 2019 in Great Britain by
Barrington Stoke Ltd
18 Walker Street, Edinburgh, EH3 7LP

www.barringtonstoke.co.uk

Text © 2019 Phil Earle
Illustrations © 2019 Steve May

A CIP catalogue record for this book is available
from the British Library upon request

ISBN: 978-1-78112-850-3

Printed in Malaysia by Times Offset

This book is super readable for young readers beginning their
independent reading journey.

CONTENTS

CHAPTER 1
WHAT A CLOD!

As the ball left Stanley's boot, the world stood still.

The grass stopped growing, the crowd stopped yelling, a small dog froze with its leg cocked against the goalpost.

This was the moment Stanley and his team had been waiting for. The moment when they would score at last. But just as the ball was about to find the corner of the net, it hit an enormous clod of earth and span at a right angle, away from the goal and out for a throw-in.

The world came alive again. Even the dog showed its disgust by breaking wind.

Stanley fell to his knees, not caring that they happened to land in the muddiest of puddles.

"Nooooooo!" he cried.

They were, without doubt, the unluckiest eleven in the whole league. Their team name was the Saints, but right now they felt like a bunch of losers.

*

It had been the same all winter.

There'd been injuries and illnesses, terrible linesman decisions, games that had been rained off when they were in the lead, plus a traffic jam that made them miss kick-off and see the game awarded to the worst team in the league.

Stanley's rotten luck today summed up the whole season. The score at the final whistle felt like a slap across the face with a soggy stinking fish.

They had lost 1–0.

Their eleventh defeat of the season. Eleven more than last year.

The Saints were devastated. And no amount of Jaffa Cakes or hot chocolate could cheer them up.

CHAPTER 2
CURSED!

"What's happened to us?" Stanley asked when the team met up for training. "I've never missed a chance that easy before."

Cal was their lightning-fast winger. "I missed an easier one," he sighed.

"Me too," said Aiden, the Saints' defensive destroyer. "The only goals

I've scored this season were in *our* net."
It was true. Just the week before, poor
Aiden had scored a freakish hat-trick of
own goals in the same match.

Hettie, their midfield dynamo, had
something to tell them. "Look at this
book I've been reading," she said. And
from her bag she pulled out a copy of
Famous Sporting Curses.

The others crowded round to have a look.

"No one goes from being the best team in the league to the worst in one single season," said Hettie. "I know what's gone wrong. We've been ... CURSED, just like some of the teams in this book."

There were gasps.

There were cries.

But the loudest noise was the laugh that came out of Stanley's mouth.

"Cursed? Are you kidding me? Curses don't really exist," he said.

But the others weren't so sure.

"How else do you explain it, Stan?" said Rafi, their tough tackler. "Last season we were beating the other teams 10–0. Now they're putting that many past us. And we can't be that bad, we just can't!"

Hettie flicked through the book and then gasped. "Oh my goodness, I've worked it out!" she said. "It's the kit. It must be."

"The kit?" said Stanley. He loved their strip. It was the best in the league, all sleek black and white stripes.

"It has to be the kit," Hettie went on. "Last season, in our old kit, we were unbeatable. This year, in the new one, we can't even shoot straight. It's not us who's cursed. It's the kit!"

"I think Hettie might be right," said Tommy.

Cal agreed.

And so did Cory.

And so did Jess. And Luca. And Rafi.
In fact, so did everyone.

Everyone except Stanley.

CHAPTER 3

WHAT IS THAT WHIFF?

The following Sunday, the Saints arrived for their next match, and Stanley had a bad feeling in his belly.

His team-mates were acting ... weird.

For starters, there was a strange whiff in the dressing room, and it seemed to be coming from Aiden.

"What *is* that smell?" Stanley asked him.

"It's garlic," Aiden told him. "I looked online and it said that the smell scares off bad spirits. So I rubbed a bit on my kit."

"A bit?! Smells like you had a bath in the stuff," said Stanley. "Plus garlic scares off vampires, you muppet. And when did we ever play against any of them?"

Aiden wasn't bothered. Instead, he took a handful of garlic cloves and shoved them down each sock. Stanley put his head in his hands.

It didn't get any better. Everyone else had thought of their own ways to counter the curse.

Cal wouldn't put on his left boot until the match started and so he had to hop through the warm-up; Tommy and Jarvis both wanted to be the last player on to the pitch and nearly ended up in a fight. As for Hettie, she wanted to wear her entire kit back to front, but the ref refused to let the game begin unless she sorted herself out.

The Saints were so busy thinking about the blasted curse that they forgot all about the most important thing – trying to win.

And as a result, everything went downhill fast.

CHAPTER 4
BUBBLING BLISTERS

The problems started in the third minute, when the lace on Cal's boot came undone. He'd done it up in such a hurry that he'd made a right old mess of his double knot.

So what? you might think. Big deal, his lace came undone. But as he turned to defend a long ball, he tripped over and

twisted his ankle. The opposing attacker
showed him no pity and raced through
to steer the ball into the bottom corner.

1–0. Dear, oh dear, oh dear.

That was it for poor Cal. His game was over, and the Saints had lost their quickest player.

"Come on," yelled Stanley. "We can get back into this. There's plenty of time."

He was right of course, but time, and luck, seemed to be on the side of the opposition.

By half-time, the Saints had used all their subs.

Tommy and Luca had headbutted each other instead of the ball and knocked themselves out. Cory had kicked the goalpost instead of the ball, wrecking his foot in the process.

As for Aiden – well, by half-time his match was over too.

The garlic had worked its own magic. "My legs are itching like mad," he moaned.

When he rolled his socks down,
Stanley saw the angriest, reddest rash
ever all over Aiden's shins.

It was like something out of a horror
movie. Aiden's legs were red and

blotchy, and there were blisters bubbling on both calves.

Aiden was tough. He could bring down a brick wall with his tackles, but when his mum saw his legs, the only place he was going was to the hospital.

Within minutes, their car was screeching out of the car park and the Saints were starting the second half two goals and two players down.

I wish I could tell you that their bad luck ended there and then.

But it didn't. Of course it didn't – there are still pages of this story left to read.

Instead, the score-line got worse. The Saints battled and tackled and sprinted, but with less than a full team, they were over-run.

By the end, even the winning team couldn't remember how many goals they'd scored.

The final whistle couldn't come quick enough, and when it did come, boy, did those Saints feel sad.

CHAPTER 5
STAN NEEDS A PLAN ...

Stanley didn't sleep that night. It wasn't so much that his team kept getting beaten all the time. What hurt was the fact that they had started to feel like losers.

They had one final game to play, and there was no way Stanley wanted to lose that too.

He was scared that if they did, no one would want to play for the Saints any more.

Stanley felt sicker than when he'd smelled the garlic wafting off Aiden's legs. He had to do something, quickly.

As he lay there, he remembered a story he'd spotted in Hettie's book. It was about an Australian team who'd asked a voodoo priest to break the curse they thought had been placed on their team.

It lit a spark in Stanley's brain – a spark that grew into a flame, which exploded into a towering inferno that filled him with hope.

Stanley still didn't believe the Saints were cursed. Not one bit. But his friends did. So if he couldn't change their minds, then maybe he could play along.

All they had to do was win a game and finish the season on a high. It was all down to him, and he didn't have much time …

CHAPTER 6
A MAGIC ELIXIR

"What are we all doing here?" Cory asked.

It *was* a bit weird. The whole team was squeezed into Stanley's tiny kitchen. It was also weird that Stanley had drawn the blinds in the middle of the day.

But what was even weirder was that Stanley was dressed ... as a wizard.

Yes, you heard right. Pointy hat (from his sister's dressing-up box), cloak (spare-room curtains) and half-moon specs (borrowed from his great-grandma).

He had even drawn a beard on in grey felt tip, but it didn't look realistic.

In fact, it looked ... well ... make your mind up for yourself.

"I've listened to you," Stanley told them now. "The kit *is* cursed. But not for long."

"So are you going to *magic* us a new kit?" Jess asked.

"Er ... not exactly. We're going to banish the curse with this magic potion ..."

Stanley waved his hands wildly and whipped a perfume bottle out from under his cloak. It was one he'd swiped from Grandma's dressing table a few hours before.

Mouths fell open and gasps fell out in wonder. Stanley would've laughed at his friends if he didn't need them to believe his story.

"Everyone put their kit on the table. I need to spray it with my elixir."

"What's it made of?" Rafi asked.

"A wizard never tells anyone his secrets," Stanley whispered. "But its ingredients come from all around the world." He wasn't lying. He'd raided the spice shelf in the larder. In his elixir, there was chilli from India, oregano from Italy, paprika from Morocco. It smelled exotic!

No one asked any more questions – they didn't even know what "elixir" meant. Even so, they quickly put their kit on the table and ten seconds later Stanley was putting phase two into action.

He dimmed the lights and started to chant as he sprayed the elixir over the football kit. Even he was impressed by the gobbledy-gook that came out of his mouth.

"Curseeeeey," he moaned. "Cursey-wursey-wooooooooo. Obbledy-bobbledy-dooooo. Spirits, begone. Woe, begone. Offsides, begone too."

Stanley paced behind his team-mates and flicked the light switch, sending the room into darkness and his team-mates into a wild mix of fear and excitement.

"It's working!" yelled Cal.

"It must be," agreed Luca.

"Stanley, you're a genius!" shouted Hettie. "We're going to win again!"

But there was no time to enjoy the glory. Suddenly the lights burst back on and there was Stanley's dad.

"Er ... hi, Pops," said Stanley. "You couldn't put the kit in the machine, could you? The final part of the process is to rinse off the last of the curse."

Dad just nodded. Whatever was going on in there, he didn't want to know about it.

CHAPTER 7
BAD TO WORSE!

Match day. The first match of the rest of their lives. Everyone was pulling on their freshly washed, curse-free kit.

"Er ... Stan ..." came a voice from inside one of the football strips. Was it Luca? It was hard to hear. "I can't quite get my shirt on."

"Me neither," came another voice, and another. Stanley looked up to see half a dozen headless corpses wrestling with football shirts that were *way* too small for them.

"I can't play in this – it doesn't fit!" yelled Tommy.

Everyone else agreed.

"Nonsense," Stanley said. He ignored the nagging worry in his chest and pulled his own shirt on. But that was all he said, as once he was wearing it he couldn't breathe, let alone speak.

All around the changing room, the problems were the same. Aiden pretended to kick a ball and the back of his shorts ripped from top to bottom. Cory's kit looked like it belonged to a mouse, not a super-striker.

"It's the curse!!!" yelled Hettie.

"*No, it's not!!!*" replied Stanley. "The kit must have shrunk in the wash, that's all."

"Well, we can't play like this," said Jess.

Stanley sighed. Jess was right. Four
of the Saints pulled him out of his shirt
and then he legged it to the store room.
Time was quickly running out.

He scanned every corner, looking for
something the team could wear. There
were corner flags and cones; there were
nets and there were bibs.

And there, in the darkest corner, was a tatty old wicker basket.

Stanley had nothing to lose, so he lifted up the lid.

What lay inside was awful. Terrible. A nightmare. The others would go potty.

But it would have to do.

CHAPTER 8

"I'M NOT WEARING THAT!"

A cry went up.

"I am not wearing that!"

"Why not? It's a kit, isn't it?" Stanley said.

"Er ..." said Luca, "it might have been once, before the moths scoffed it!"

"OK, so it's old, but at least it is a Saints kit." Stanley tried to sound as if he knew what he was talking about.

The shirt *was* black and white, but it had pointy collars as long as elephants' ears and a drawstring that zigzagged across the chest and neck.

The shorts were little better. They were *huge* – so baggy you could've hidden six badgers up each leg.

The socks weren't too bad, though they had been attacked by the moths too and smelled like nothing he'd ever smelled before.

"That's it," sighed Cory. "I'm not playing. We're cursed and this kit proves it. I'm quitting."

Others made similar noises. Suddenly, stamp collecting and knitting felt more fun than football.

"Please don't quit!" Stanley pleaded. "Think of all the matches we've won over the years. All the times we've fought back. I know we'll look a bit daft, but if we can win wearing this, we can win in anything!"

No one looked convinced.

"Please," said Stanley. "Just give it until half-time. And if we really can't go on, then we'll call it off. Please?"

There was a group sigh, followed by a series of grumpy "OK"s and "Fine"s.

The Saints pulled on their kit, tied up their laces and trudged onto the pitch, laughter ringing in their ears from everyone who saw them.

CHAPTER 9

QUITTING TIME

The game started.

Stanley breathed a sigh of relief. But two minutes in, his belief was about to be tested.

Rafi picked up the ball and tore down the wing. Stanley held his breath as he swung a cross in.

Cory leaped into the air, ready to scissor-kick the ball into the top corner. But as the cross reached him, there was a loud noise and a black blur as something shot from Cory and into the net like a rocket.

The Saints cheered and raced to celebrate. But Cory wasn't in the mood for dancing. He knew that what had ended up in the net wasn't the ball but his shorts.

The ancient elastic in them had snapped, and they'd twanged clean off his legs and past the goalkeeper.

If only the ball had done the same.

It wasn't a good sign, and they weren't the only shorts to misbehave.

By half-time, three more pairs had twanged to their death, while Hettie had almost taken off like a balloon when a strong gust of wind took hold of her.

It was a wonder the other team could play for laughing, but somehow they managed and by half-time the Saints found themselves two goals down.

It was a very unhappy dressing room. Pretty much everyone was ready to quit.

"I've had enough!"

"I'm going home!"

Stanley tried and tried but, no matter what he did, he couldn't stop his friends from believing in this stupid curse.

He was so fed up that he felt he had no option but to quit too. But just as he was peeling off his shirt, he had a glimmer of a thought. Maybe he should be more like his friends? Maybe he should believe in stories just like they did? Maybe, if he did, he could play it to his advantage ...

Jumping to his feet and tucking his shirt back into his shorts, he launched into one final plan ...

CHAPTER 10

STANLEY PLAYS A BLINDER

"There's something I need to tell you," Stanley shouted.

"What? That you've got rubbish taste in kit?" Aiden shouted back. "Tell us something we don't already know."

But Stanley wasn't going to be put off. "Oh, this kit isn't rubbish," he said. "Far from it. I wasn't going to tell you, because you know I don't believe all this curse nonsense, but this kit ... well, it might be old, but it's special."

Everyone groaned.

"It's true! This kit was worn by the Saints fifty years ago, and for the two

seasons they wore it, they never lost a game. In fact, they barely conceded a goal."

Hettie was the first to show interest. "Really? Who wore my shirt?"

Stanley started to sweat. He hadn't expected questions, but he couldn't stop now. He had to make something up. And fast.

"Number seven? Hmm, who was it? Oh yes, a girl called Elsie had that strip. She made more tackles in one game than most people managed in a whole year!"

Hettie smiled as she looked down at her shirt.

"What about mine?" asked Cory.

Stanley didn't hesitate.

"Nine was worn by a boy called Lennon. The greatest centre-forward the club ever had seen. Scored at least ninety goals a season until he turned professional at the age of sixteen. Ended up playing for England, I think."

Cory liked the sound of that.

Questions followed from every player, and Stanley had to think answers up for each and every one of them. He invented towering centre-halves, lightning-fast wingers and super-tough full-backs. By the time he'd finished, each of his team-mates couldn't wait to get back out on that pitch and show that they had the same skills as the boys and girls who had worn their strip half a century ago.

Stanley ran out feeling something he hadn't felt for quite some time.

He felt confident.

CHAPTER 11

A GAME OF TWO HALVES

The Saints were now like a different team, which was crazy, because nothing had changed. Apart from the fact that now they were full of belief.

They ran and chased and tackled and crossed. They headed and trapped and sprinted and passed.

"Keep battling!" yelled Stanley. "There's a goal just round the corner."

He was right. At last, after great work from Cal, the ball was bundled home by Cory.

The Saints celebrated like they'd won the World Cup, but Stanley was having none of it.

"Come on," he shouted, "five minutes left and we're still one down."

That was all the Saints needed to hear. Within seconds Hettie had spotted the keeper off his line and hit the cheekiest of lobs, which span perfectly into the net.

The Saints smelled victory and now they pinned the other team in their own half.

Some slick play from Aiden and Luca allowed Rafi to slip the ball to Stanley. The edge of the box was right in front of him, but just as he was about to make contact, he felt his legs go from under him as a defender tripped him up. "FOUL!" went the cry, and the referee agreed. He awarded the Saints a free kick from the edge of the box.

Talk about a last-minute chance!

But oddly enough, all of a sudden nobody wanted to take the free kick.

"Why don't you take it, Stan?" said Cory. "You found the lucky kit. If it wasn't for you, we'd be ten down by now."

Stanley's heart thudded. After all, he knew the story of the kit was just that –

a story. But at the same time he knew that this was his chance to do something great for the team.

This was his chance to make it a season to remember. So he marked out his run-up and stared at the ball.

Hit the target, he thought, *that's all you can do ...*

The ref blew his whistle.

Stanley took a deep breath and danced forward, his laces making the sweetest contact.

Once again the world stood still. The grass stopped growing, the crowd stopped yelling, a small dog froze with its leg cocked against the goalpost.

Over the wall the ball span, on and on until ... crack! It walloped the crossbar and fell down, right onto the goal line.

"No!" cried Stanley, but his despair turned to joy as the ball span slowly back ... into ... the ... net.

He'd done it! Scored the most miraculous goal with the last kick of the game.

The celebrations went on and on, long after they'd shaken hands with their opponents, lasting well into the end-of-season party at the local milkshake shack.

"We *have* to play in this kit next year too!" said Hettie, with a grin.

"And the year after that," added Cory.

"For as long as we play for the Saints!" shouted Aiden.

But Stanley just slurped at his shake. He knew full well that the kit wouldn't fit them next season, and he knew that there was nothing magic about it either.

But he kept quiet. Why spoil the moment?

They were the Saints – the Lucky Eleven – and Stanley wouldn't have it any other way.

With thanks to the real Saints!

Ronnie	Cory
Calan	Leon
Finlay	Gabriel
Rowan	Jarvis
Fred	Tommy
Luca	Ottis
Jess	Lucas
Kylan	Benji
Raffi	Ethan
Max	Lennon
Aiden	Matthew
Stan	Sam
Hettie	Jack
Sid	

Our books are tested
for children and young people by
children and young people.

Thanks to everyone who consulted on
a manuscript for their time and effort in
helping us to make our books better
for our readers.